GOOD NEWS! BAD NEWS!

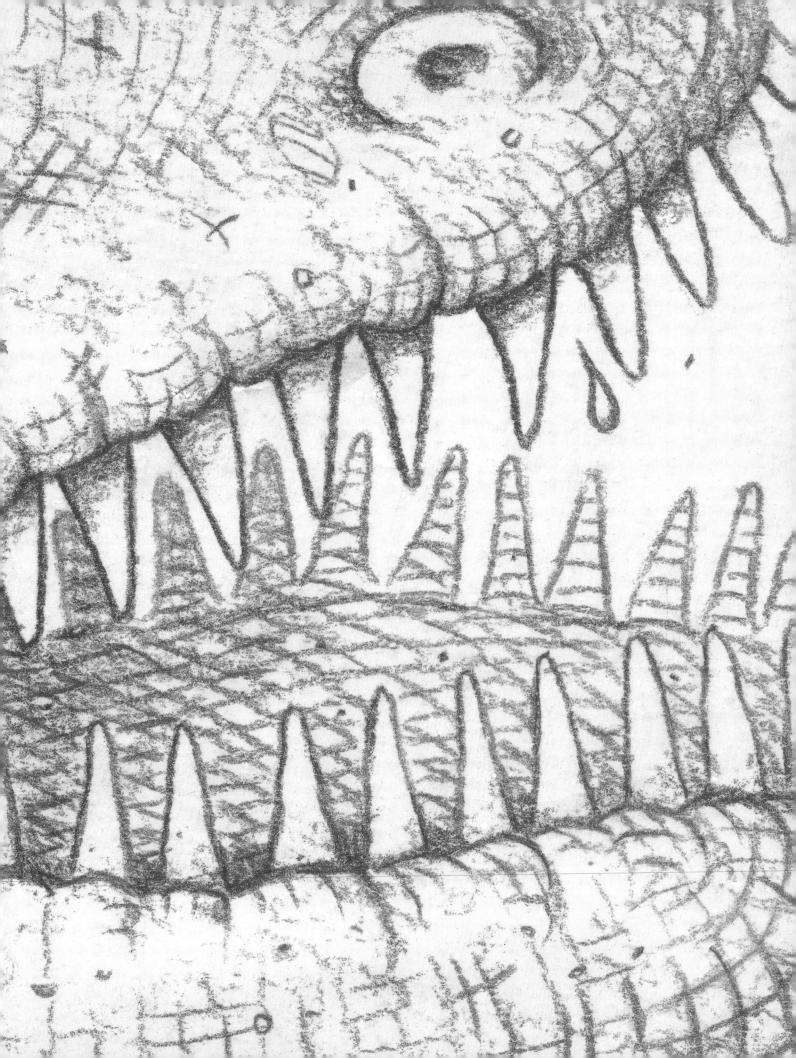

For Joe and Millie

First published in hardback in
Great Britain by HarperCollins Publishers Ltd in 2001
First published in paperback by Collins Picture Books in 2002

1 3 5 7 9 10 8 6 4 2
ISBN: 0-00-664772-3

Collins Picture Books is an imprint of the Children's Division, part of HarperCollins Publishers Ltd.
Text and illustrations copyright © Colin McNaughton 2001
The author/illustrator asserts the moral right to be identified as the author/illustrator of the work.
A CIP catalogue record for this title is available from the British Library.
The HarperCollins website address is:
www.**fire**and**water**.com

Printed in Hong Kong

Colin McNaughton

Collins

An imprint of HarperCollinsPublishers

Good news! It's a beautiful day. Hooray!

Bad news! It's a school day. Boo!

Good news!
You've
got the
day off.
Hooray!

Bad news!
To go
to the
dentist.
Boo!

Go!

Bad news!
You meet *those* girls.
Boo!

Good news!
One of your
teachers comes by.
Hooray!

Bad news!
The one who doesn't like you.
Boo!

Bad news!
By aliens.
Boo!

Good news!
They're friendly.
Hooray!

Bad news!
They smell like babies' nappies.
Poo!

Good news!
They let you go.
Hooray!

Bad news!
Without a parachute.
Boo!

Good news!
You land on something soft.
Hooray!

Bad news!
A big hairy monster.
Boo!

Good news!
Something chases him off.
Hooray!

Bad news!
A herd of elephants.
Boo!

Good news!
They get chased off.
Hooray!

Bad news!
By a Tyrannosaurus Rex.
Boo!

Good news!
You're saved just in time.
Hooray!

Bad news!
By a witch.
Boo!

Good news!
You jump from the
witch's broomstick.
Hooray!

Bad news!
You land on your
dentist's head.
Boo!

Good news!
He's not hurt.
Hooray!

Bad news!
You're just in time for your dental appointment.
Boo!

Good news!
It doesn't hurt a bit.
Hooray!

Bad news!
Your dentist is
Count Dracula.
Boo!

Good news!
You escape and
reach home safely.
Hooray!

Bad news!
There *is* no more
bad news.
Hooray!

Sensational books by
Colin McNaughton

Whatever you do...

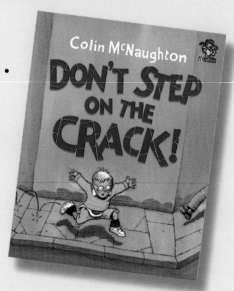

Colin McNaughton explores, with characteristic wit and exuberance, the possible dangers of ignoring this familiar lore of childhood. Bursting with colour, *Don't Step on the Crack!* is guaranteed to feed the imagination and ensure a simple walk along the street will never be the same again...

hardback 0-00-198417-9   paperback 0-00-664771-5

"Tingle with anticipation at each imminent new horror – classic Colin McNaughton."
Practical Parenting

Have you read all the **Preston Pig** stories?

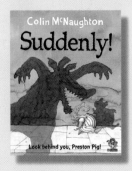

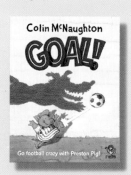

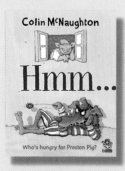

0-00-714013-4   0-00-714011-8   0-00-714014-2   0-00-714015-0   0-00-714012-6

Colin McNaughton is one of Britain's most highly-acclaimed picture book talents and a winner of many prestigious awards. His Preston Pig stories are hugely successful with Preston now starring in his own animated television series on CITV.

NEW!
Colin McNaughton
Oomph!
Fall in love with Preston Pig!
0-00-712635-2